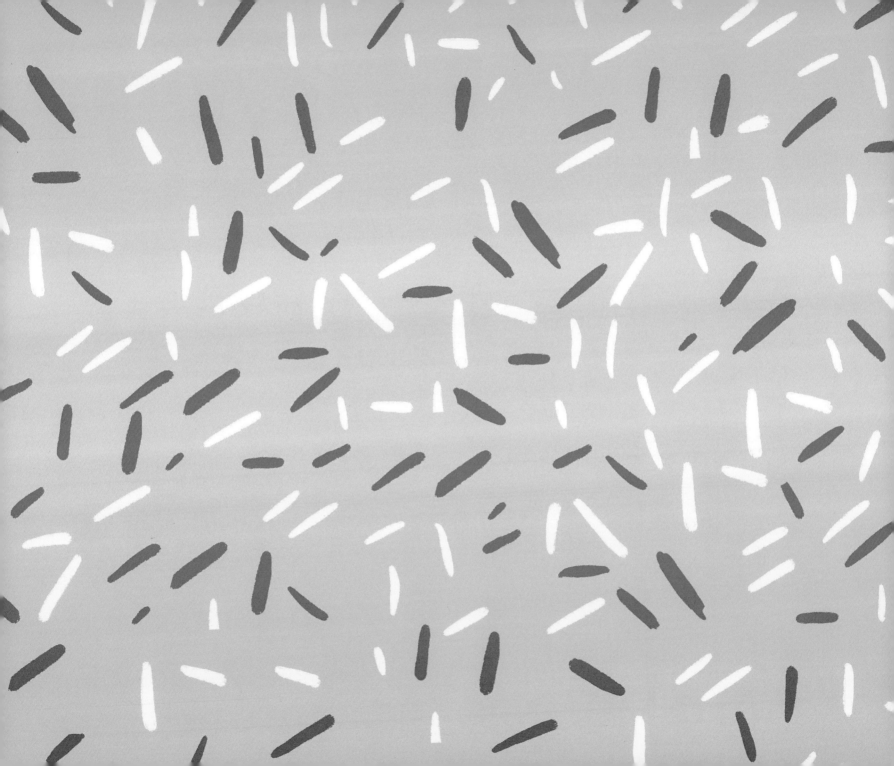

To my family and friends for easing my worries.
You know who you are. —C.J.

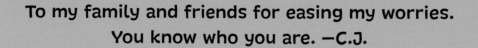

Donut Worry is published by Capstone Editions,
an imprint of Capstone
1710 Roe Crest Drive
North Mankato, Minnesota 56003
www.capstonepub.com

Cataloging-in-Publication Data is available on the Library of Congress website.
ISBN: 978-1-68446-073-1(library binding)
ISBN: 978-1-68446-074-8 (eBook PDF)

Summary: Donut learns how to deal with all of her anxieties
and worries with the help of her new friend, Cookie.

Photo Credits: Shutterstock: GregoryL, Igor_83, topseller
Designer: Ted Williams

Printed and bound in China. 4205

DONUT WORRY

by Christianne Jones

illustrated by
Jack Viant

CAPSTONE EDITIONS
a capstone imprint

Summer. A time to relax and unwind and have fun . . .

. . . until August. That's when the school worries start to creep in.
And when the worries creep in, they're hard to push out.

With each passing day, Donut's worries grew. Soon they took over her life. Sometimes Donut didn't even know what she was worried about.

But she couldn't stop worrying. Her stomach hurt all the time. She couldn't eat. She couldn't sleep. Sometimes it felt like she couldn't even breathe!

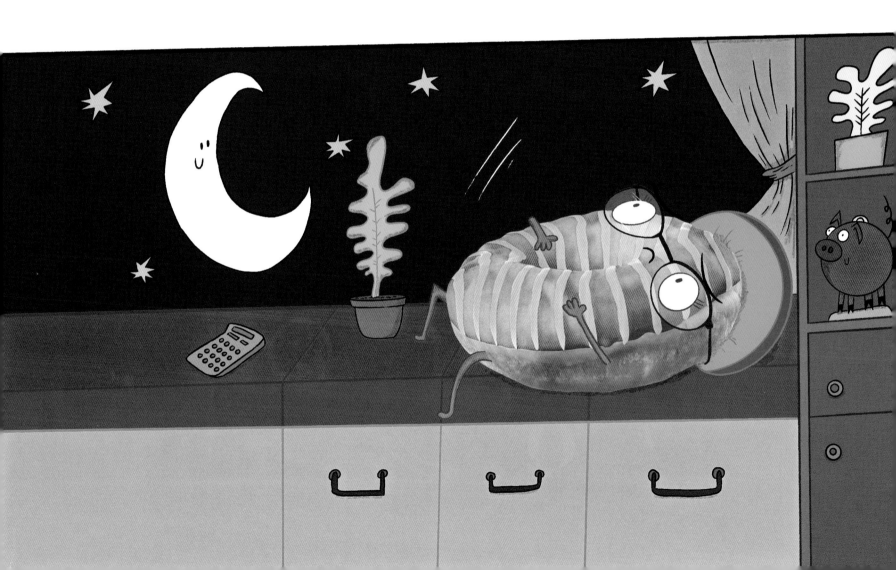

While her friends enjoyed sleepovers . . .

. . . and swimming . . .

Donut stayed home worrying.
"Don't worry!" her friends would say.

Being worried all the time was terrible. But having everyone tell her not to worry was even worse!

At Donut's family reunion, that's all she heard from everyone— over and over again!

"It wasn't easy," Cookie replied.
"I tried everything.

I went to therapy.

I wrote mantras.

"I CAN DO THIS!" MMMMAYBE NOT . . .

"WORK HARD." NOT TODAY!

"I WILL BE OKAY!!!" OR WILL I?

"TAKE ON TODAY!" NAH!

I meditated.

I exercised.

I cried.

The list goes on and on."

Donut and Cookie walked and talked and talked and walked until the sun set.

They talked about big worries. They talked about little worries. They talked about how sometimes they didn't even know what they were worried about.

When they said goodbye, Cookie told Donut something she would never forget.

It's okay not to be okay.

That night, Donut listed ways to tackle her worries.
There were lots of things she could try. She even
wrote her own mantra.

DANCE

FUN

BREATHE

CHESS

You got This!
I CAN Do This!

Every day Donut practiced new ways to conquer her worries.

Some worked. Some didn't.
But she kept trying.

Donut barely slept the night before
school started. But she was okay.

WILL MY FRIENDS BE IN MY CLASS?

IT'S OKAY IF THEY AREN'T.

WILL I LIKE MY TEACHER?

WHAT HAPPENS IF I GET SICK AT SCHOOL?

IT'S OKAY IF YOU DON'T.

WHAT HAPPENS IF I GET HURT AT RECESS?

WHAT HAPPENS IF MY BACKPACK ZIPPER GETS STUCK!

WHAT IF I HAVE TO GO TO THE BATHROOM AND IT'S NOT TIME FOR A BATHROOM BREAK?!

IT'S OKAY TO ASK THE TEACHER.

As Donut left her house the next morning, she was still worried. But she grabbed her backpack, silently repeated her mantra, took a deep breath, and smiled. She would be okay.

WORK YOUR WORRIES

It's not always easy to stop your worries from taking over. Thankfully there are lots of ways to tackle them. Donut used a mantra to help with her worries. Donut's mantra might help you too. Or try one of the exercises below.

Bubble Breathing: Pretend you have a bottle of bubbles. Breathe in through your nose as you bring the imaginary bubble wand to your mouth, thinking of one of your worries. Now blow out through your mouth, blowing that worry bubble away until it pops.

Flower and Candle Breathing: Breathe in as if you are smelling a flower. Then breathe out like you are blowing out birthday candles.

Write It Down/Tear It Up: Write down all your worries on a piece of paper. Then tear that paper into tiny pieces and throw it away.

Move It: Any kind of movement helps your body release worries. Take a walk. Do jumping jacks. Practice yoga. Run in place.

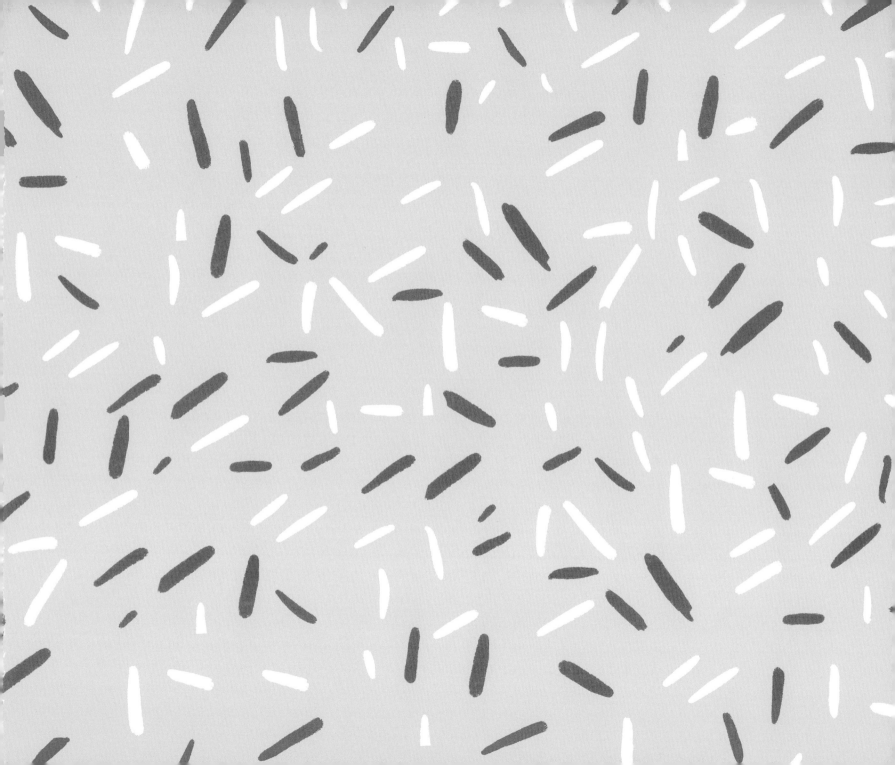